THE SOUTH & SOUTH WEST

First published in Great Britain in 2010 by
Young Writers, Remus House, Coltsfoot Drive,
Peterborough, PE2 9JX
Tel (01733) 890066 Fax (01733) 313524
Website: www.youngwriters.co.uk

Disclaimer
Young Writers has maintained every effort
to publish stories that will not cause offence.
Any stories, events or activities relating to individuals
should be read as fictional pieces and not construed
as real-life character portrayal.

Foreword

Since Young Writers was established in 1990, our aim has been to promote and encourage written creativity amongst children and young adults. By giving aspiring young authors the chance to be published, Young Writers effectively nurtures the creative talents of the next generation, allowing their confidence and writing ability to grow.

With our latest fun competition, *The Adventure Starts Here ...*, primary school children nationwide were given the tricky challenge of writing a story with a beginning, middle and an end in just fifty words.

The diverse and imaginative range of entries made the selection process a difficult but enjoyable task with stories chosen on the basis of style, expression, flair and technical skill. A fascinating glimpse into the imaginations of the future, we hope you will agree that this entertaining collection is one that will amuse and inspire the whole family.

Contents

Streatham & Clapham High School, London

Truro High School, Truro

The Mini Sagas

The Dark, Dark Jungle

One day in a dark jungle it was quiet with tired
animals. One stormy day the tiger woke up
and roared because he could not go to sleep.
When he roared all of the animals woke up and
cried because they heard a loud roar. The storm
started to stop.

Khadijah Aima (7)
Cayley Primary School, London

The Shark And The Boy

John was going home but he stopped to look at the waves in the ocean. Then a shark said, 'Yum, yum.' The shark was waiting until the boy was asleep, the boy was still awake! The shark got bored then he planned something and ate him all.

Tawheed Uddin (8)

Cayley Primary School, London

The Scariest Doll In The Whole World

Once there lived a boy called Tom. He had a
monster doll. The monster's name was Spooky.
He had horns like bulls and he had fur all over
his body. He also had prickles all over his back.
He was the most scariest doll in the whole wide
world.

Mohammed Khalid (8)
Cayley Primary School, London

Football

Once there was a football player, he was called
Chelsea. He got a penalty then the whistle was
about to blow. Chelsea scored a goal. Everyone
shouted, 'Yeahhh!' Manchester won the game.
Chelsea was very excited and very happy.

Tanvir Ahmed (7)

Cayley Primary School, London

A Dark Stormy Night

It was a dark and stormy night. There was a man
waiting and watching. He knocked on the door.
There were ghosts with him, he was frightened.
The man who knocked on the door was really
scared ...

Yasirah Jannah (8)
Cayley Primary School, London

Jake's Surprise Birthday

Jake opened the door and it was dark. No one was in the house. Jake shook his legs - he saw something move in the cupboard. He opened it. Out jumped his parents. Jake said, 'This is the best birthday ever.' Jake was so happy.

Nihal Uddin (8)
Cayley Primary School, London

Gone Is The Wolf

'Ooo wooo!' the hypnotizing werewolf cried, like
blood his eyes turned a sickening red.
'Stop crying!' the moon opened its secret mouth.
As fast as a thunderbolt, the wolf jumped back.
Out of nowhere the moon took a humungous
bite ... and swallowed the terrible wolf. Gone was
the wolf.

Halema Ogazi-Khan (11)
Gladstone Park Primary School, London

Beware

Coolgirl7: Bored nothin' to do, u?
Monkeyfan3: Wat? Heard something.
Coolgirl7: check out!
Monkeyfan3: Na, too scared!
Coolgirl7: Be brave, not a wimp lol!
Monkeyfan3: Na later!
Coolgirl7: Mum/Dad/Sis?
Monkeyfan3: All out.
Coolgirl7: Check it? Hurry!
Monkeyfan3: K, one sec!
10 mins later ... *Monkeyfan3 offline ... !*

Retaj Layes (11)
Gladstone Park Primary School, London

Untitled

Badboy92: I'm watching Disney Channel. *Sotuff88: sme.* Badboy92: who's at home? *Sotuff88: me and my sis, u?* Badboy92: home alone. *Sotuff88: kl.* Badboy92: OMG! Someone is banging in one of the rooms. *Sotuff88: go and check!* Badboy92: OK, BRB! *Sotuff88: stop being silly, now are you there?* Badboy92: *offline.*

Sona Halai (11)
Gladstone Park Primary School, London

9

Offline Man

Blandenxl: Mum there's someone online
that I don't know! Mum are you even there?
Mario1717: I'll kill you if you call Mum. Blandenxl:
how come you're offline and you're talking to
me? *Mario1717: I'm behind you.* Blandenxl: argh!
Mario1717: you can no longer call your mum.

Sandalu Suraweera (11)

Gladstone Park Primary School, London

Online Kid

'Ooh there's someone online'
Mario123: Hi Blazererxl.
Blazererxl: Do you know that boy in school?
Mario123: Yes, he's nasty.
Blazererxl: The refrigerator opened by itself.
Mario123: Go and check it out.
Blazererxl: The door creaked open.
Mario123: Not again.
Blazererxl: Bye!
Mario123: Bye!

Anis Boutejdir (11)
Gladstone Park Primary School, London

Best Friend Vanishes!

Before I decided to go to bed my gran read me
a story. I started to feel like this story was going
to happen to me. The very next day I went to
Sarena's house. I rang and rang the doorbell but
no one answered? Where was everyone?

Denise Warner (10)
Gladstone Park Primary School, London

Caught Out!

Bin2: Hi Ed98. *Ed98: Hi.* Bin2: You see that boy at school? *Ed98: Yeah.* Bin2: You his friend? *Ed98: No!* Bin2: Why? *Ed98: He's odd and boring plus weird, dumb, rubbish at football. Why aren't you talking?* Bin2: I'm Joe. Thanks a lot.

Jermaine Attah (11)
Gladstone Park Primary School, London

The Babysitter From Planet Evil Crisis

'Argh!' shrieked Stan.
'What's up?' said Steve panicking.
'It's the babysitter ... she's coming! Lock the doors!'
'I can't, I don't know where the keys are!'
'Fattie the babysitter is at the door! Oh good precious God help us please!'
'I've got some tomatoes to throw!'
'Ketchup!'
'Fire!'
'*Oops*, hi Mum?'

Micah Sylvan
Gladstone Park Primary School, London

14

The Everlasting Cry

Coolgal70: I'm going to that lake.
PrincessJo09: : (Scary, I'm frightened.
Coolgal70: But I saw something, need to go
back …
Both: *offline* …
Five minutes later at the lake … they arrived.
Unfortunately to their amazement there was
nothing there. Before long, Coolgal70 had gone.
Where had she gone … ?
'Argh!'

Desai Callum-Clarke (11)
Gladstone Park Primary School, London

Halloween

Badboy7: Hi. *Coolboy2: Hi, do you like girls?*
Badboy7: Nah, they are too rude. *Coolboy2:*
Anyways, have you watched yesterday's match,
Man U vs AC? Badboy7: Yeah Man U won 4-nil.
Coolboy2: OMG. Badboy7: What happened?
Coolboy2: The door is open. Badboy7: Go check.
15 minutes later … *Coolboy2: offline.*

Mukhtar Mohamed (11)
Gladstone Park Primary School, London

The Voice!

Rose was annoyingly bored. Suddenly she heard footsteps, she shuddered. Gasping she edged towards the door. 'Rose come to me!' a gruff voice boomed. Rose's waterworks turned on. 'Please!' she squealed. The door creaked open, making Rose leap back to reveal ... her brother in a mask. 'You idiot!'
'Ha!'

Haleema Ogazi-Khan (11)
Gladstone Park Primary School, London

Robber!

Slowly, John approached the door. He peered inside. There was nobody home. He snuck in. He took the car keys. Then he crept upstairs. He heard a ticking sound. *Tick tock!* John tiptoed into the bedroom. He took the house keys. Suddenly he heard the door open. 'John, you home?'

Sebastian Swiderski (10)

Gladstone Park Primary School, London

What Was It?

I was puzzled. I stepped in ... I saw a red trail
along the floor. What was it? I felt petrified. I
clamped the rail; took step by step. *Tip tap.*
I approached the end of the trail, my heart
stopped. In the corner, there was my dog seizing
tomato ketchup.

Hema Mistry (11)
Gladstone Park Primary School, London

Untitled

I ran, my heart pounding like a thousand drums.
Dreaded beast charging behind. It was catching
up. I knew I'd have to surrender. *No!* I wouldn't
give up. *Bam!* Falling smack on the concrete floor.
The horrid creature gained on me. I sighed. I'd
have to get the next bus.

Tea Simei-Cunningham (10)
Gladstone Park Primary School, London

Untitled

Ferociously the water seized Ria. Ria took a breath; she couldn't breathe. She screeched but could she be heard in the vast water? Exhausted, she stopped struggling. She admitted she was going to drown. However, she heard something ... the instructor was telling her, 'Come out the pool!'

Tatum Marrie (10)
Gladstone Park Primary School, London

Man Stalker

We were on a trip. Entering the luscious scents
of the forest, we heard patting footsteps getting
closer and closer ... Out of the blue a wrinkly
hand touched my shoulder! Then, the hairs on my
back stood up. Suddenly, a deep voice groaned,
'Can you tell me the way out?'

Jasmine Franklin (11)
Gladstone Park Primary School, London

The Woodcutter

The woodcutter glared at the jury. He was livid.
'Let me go!' he roared. Little Red Riding Hood
stood up and defended her lover. She loved the
woodcutter. Suddenly the doors opened. Quick
as a flash, Little Red and the woodcutter left.
'We've got Grandma, also we're getting married.'
Oops!

Ayub Abdi (11)
Gladstone Park Primary School, London

Untitled

Gradually I dragged myself to the front door.
Then as I pulled my key out, I noticed that the
door was open. *Why?* Shivering, I pushed the
rusty door. It was pitch-black. *Where are my
parents?* Squinting, I stared at a dark figure.
Suddenly the lights switched on ...
'Surprise!'

Aleena Majeed (10)
Gladstone Park Primary School, London

The World War

Bang, crash, wallop! A bomb flew past my head.
There and then I knew WWII had started! *Was
it really happening ... ?* Fog was everywhere.
I couldn't even see the path in front of me.
A warning bell rang. All of a sudden I heard a
chuckle ...
'Cut! Everyone off set!'

Josephine Mensah (11)
Gladstone Park Primary School, London

The Disaster Of 9/11

Boom! Crash! Bang! The Boeing 747 collided into the tip of the towering skyscraper. Creating a dent, the plane hung on by the skin of its teeth. A blanket of grey smoke covered New York. Everyone in despair. Screaming filled the atmosphere. There was silence. *Was I dreaming?* Yes! Sleeping.

Cherise Pacquette (11)

Gladstone Park Primary School, London

A Saga

My teacher Miss Prior is asking me to write a flaming saga. How can I write one with approximately 50 words! The head Mr Bruce can't do that! Erm, I think I'm writing one, yes, I am. How thick. Well I think Mr Bruce will be happy.

Sadek Al-Alawy (10)
Gladstone Park Primary School, London

Untitled

Shocked, everybody froze ... Suddenly he was
embarrassed. Red was dripping from his shirt,
the shop stood still as everyone was shocked.
He needed to ask for another Big Mac as the one
he just had, the ketchup went all over his shirt!
There you go, fifty words, a saga, surprised?

Khuluud Hussein (10)
Gladstone Park Primary School, London

Untitled

Splash! I couldn't see a thing. Was it a mermaid?
I dived in ... there was a girl staring at me. She
had an evil smile on her face. The girl nudged me,
she took me to Atlantis, the lost city. Everything
started to fade quickly. Was it all a dream?

Maryam-Hani Ali (10)
Gladstone Park Primary School, London

Untitled

Creak, the door rapidly opened. 'Haaaa!' people yelling everywhere. As I cautiously stepped in I could see blood dripping off someone's hand who was approaching me ... Without thinking twice I darted upstairs. Suddenly ... I caught sight of a perilous skeleton. Was I going to survive? Oh it was Halloween!

Igor Da Silva (11)

Gladstone Park Primary School, London

Ghostly Things Were Going On

As Margret entered the ghostly house she found herself creeping behind a ghost. Ghostly things were going on in the haunted house. Before time got on Margret found a door. Behind that door the lights were off and as Margret stepped through her family were there. 'Happy birthday Margret!'

Jordan Raymond (11)
Gladstone Park Primary School, London

Humpty-Dumpty In My Own Words

Eggy Dumpty got thrown over a wall 50 feet
high. Eggy Dumpty fell to the ground and wished
he could fly. Eggy Dumpty cracked his head so
Eggy Dumpty's mum sent him to bed. All Eggy
Dumpty's family and his dad couldn't put him
back, so now they're sad!

Mohammed Sultan (11)

Gladstone Park Primary School, London

Big Green Gruesome Girl

Once upon a time there lived a gruesome girl, big,
green, grim girl. One day her mum told her to go
to the forest to chop a tree and put her bogies
in the tree trunk, then put the tree back on top.
Suddenly she saw a million wolves! *Argh!*

Sarmad Kayani Khan (11)
Gladstone Park Primary School, London

Medusa, The Ugly Old Hag

Medusa, the old hag, was a monster who was so ugly. With one look you would die because she was so ugly. It is thought that they threw her down to Earth. Until one day she met a man who was very ugly because somehow he managed to kill her!

Ganiyu Amstel (11)
Gladstone Park Primary School, London

A Girl Called Saga

One sunny day a girl called Saga was at home eating crisps. She decided to go to her pretty room. Then amazingly she saw her cute puppy smoking a cigarette. 'Wow,' she said and then finished her crisps. She went downstairs and played on her black PS3.

Stephanie Bankole (11)
Gladstone Park Primary School, London

Wiggle And Woggle

Wiggle went down the hill to Woggle. He knocked on the door; nothing happened. He went up the hill to his house. After Wiggle decided to go to Woggle; Woggle decided to go to Wiggle. Wiggle was halfway to Woggle's; he saw Woggle. Suddenly they started to fight.

Mohammed Elius Habibzadeh (11)
Gladstone Park Primary School, London

How Are You?

'Hello, my name is Abdullah.'
'How are you?'
'I am fine thank you.'
'I go to GPPS from 9.00 to 3.15, it's fun at school,
I like it.'
'Do you?'
'We do maths, literacy and a lot more. We have
break and lunch too. It's great fun. See you.'

Abdullah Qayoumi (10)
Gladstone Park Primary School, London

Untitled

Yes sir, yes sir, I can see, but it is the same with
me. Let's hug each other and say goodbye. Bring
back other magnificent memories, when we used
to lie. I told my mum I will never, ever drink, and I
will never slyly wink. Wire bends, story ends.

Khaliyl Queensborough (11)
Gladstone Park Primary School, London

Medusa The Gorgon

Medusa the revolting Gorgon killed people by
turning them into stone. One day Perseus, a hero,
told the King he'd kill her and then he would get
half of the King's land. So he got his shield and
went to her swamp. He shone the shield on her
ugly face.

Rahul Hirani (10)

Gladstone Park Primary School, London

Little Sparkle

Little Sparkle flies so high like an emerald in the sky, looking for her mummy. Just say hey, on the bright blue Milky Way. Another big, bright silver star coming to play, hooray. Little Sparkle flies so high like an emerald in the bright blue sky. Night, night, bedtime!

Kanice Pyne (11)
Gladstone Park Primary School, London

Minngle, Minngle Show Me Your Snoozing Time

Minngle, minngle magnificent moon who glows
its shimmering light on us. Oh I wonder how you
snooze, like an apple on a twig running as fast as a
star for his supper. Minngle, Minngle magnificent
moon, oh I wonder how you snooze, maybe even
like an angry dad snoring snap.

Alina Kiyani (11)
Gladstone Park Primary School, London

The Duck And The Cow

A duck and a cow were going to go to a funfair, they were going to go on a roller coaster. But then the sheep came and told them, 'Don't go on that ride.' But the cow and the duck never listened. So then they sadly died.

Ummaqulsoom Hussain (11)
Gladstone Park Primary School, London

A Twist In The Tail

There once was a dragon. He wanted to be rich so his dad said to climb on the stairs to the dragon's lair. He saw him doing exercise and had a chat. He chopped his head and he died because the head dropped onto him! He suffocated on the blood.

Javahn Gordon (11)
Gladstone Park Primary School, London

Baby In The Night

Angrily, Linda woke up to the sound of her baby crying. She walked into the hallway, nightgown swinging round her ankles. The crying carried on as she walked. She swung the door open. She gaped as she peered upon her baby. There was her child, drinking cold, sharp vodka!

Adelaide Hill (10)
Gladstone Park Primary School, London

The Alleyway

Walking through the alleyway, the girl strolled back home. She sighed with anxiety. Unexpectedly a shadow cast over her. A shiver of fear surged through her body. As she jogged, the surreptitious shadow was lurking over her. Panting, heavily, a hand tapped her. 'You forgot your change,' smiled the shopkeeper.

Jodie Lee (10)
Gladstone Park Primary School, London

Humpty-Dumpty And The Farting Tiger

Curiously Humpty-Dumpty went into the cave,
unfortunately he got washed by the wave. Braver
than a bolt he came inside, he saw a tiger farting
behind. He thought the tiger was really dumb.
The tiger angrily bit his bum. The tiger knocked
his head, unfortunately he was sadly dead.

Mohamed Abdulrahman (10)
Gladstone Park Primary School, London

Clumsy Humpty's Death Fall

Clumsy Humpty climbed up a wall. Suddenly he tumbled down, knocked his head on a golden wall. Every villager, woman and man, decided to send Humpty to hospital where the doctors tried to put Humpty back together. Unfortunately it did not work. So they put old Humpty to bed forever.

Dana Walsh (10)
Gladstone Park Primary School, London

Tom's Garden

Tom likes taking care of his garden and he never
lets anyone go there.
One night he heard a rustling sound in his garden
so he went to see what it was. Then he saw it
was a bush so he went back to bed.

Jasmine Francis
Gladstone Park Primary School, London

Party Boy

One day there was a wealthy man. His name was
Turkenton. He lived in a mansion. He had a plane
runway and two pets - one tiger and a gorilla.
He lived in Barbados. His plane was an AC130
and a care package plane. He always flew around
Barbados having fun.

Morgan Williams (10)
Grampound-With-Creed CE School, Truro

Being Late For Work

Mike Time was always angry because he was always late for work. He went and bought a massive alarm clock from Argos. He put it right next to his bed. He was never late for work again which made him very happy. He got his job back!

Shaun Beckett (10)

Grampound-With-Creed CE School, Truro

Jonty's Adventures

The army approached the time portal. It sucked them in and they found themselves in the Death Star. 'Wow,' said Jonty. Suddenly they heard the droids coming. 'Attack!' said Jonty. Darth Vader attacked Jonty. *Bang!* A bomb went off. 'Yay,' said Jonty.

Then Dave yelled, 'I found the portal.'

Jack Bennett (9)
Grampound-With-Creed CE School, Truro

The Refrigerator Of Hell

Once upon a time in Ted's house, Ted wanted a can of cola. He went into the kitchen and he opened the fridge door. There were no cans of cola. Suddenly the fridge door slammed shut. Some red evil eyes popped out of the fridge and locked him in.

Miles Pender (8)

Grampound-With-Creed CE School, Truro

Aeroplane Chaos

Once upon a time a crazy axe man robbed a fast jet plane that Wayne Rooney was on. The axe man tried to kill him but Rooney kicked a football and he fell out of the window and died. He landed in a smelly ditch by the A30.

Finn Birnie (10)
Grampound-With-Creed CE School, Truro

Dinosaurs' Mountain!

On a bright sunny day a dinosaur was eating grass when another dinosaur appeared. They began to fight and one fell off the mountain. 'Oh no, are you OK?'
'I'm fine but can we both live on this mountain?'
The dinosaurs became friends and they were happy to share.

Chloe Carbin (9)
Locking Primary School, Weston-super-Mare

The Sea Monster

It was a lovely sunny day. We went to the beach. I couldn't wait to take a swim, and ran down to the sea. After a while, I saw something big swimming towards me. It was scary. It looked like a monster, '*Argh!*' Phew! It was only my dad.

James Waite (9)

Locking Primary School, Weston-super-Mare

Snowstorm

James was the only child left outside in the terrible snowstorm. He couldn't see where he was going at all. He kept walking through the storm. James saw a ladder and climbed up. He pushed a button at the top and the snow disappeared. Then the sun shone.

James Elvey (8)
Locking Primary School, Weston-super-Mare

It's Easter!

One Easter Day a girl woke up and looked in her
mother's room and found that she wasn't there.
She looked outside. Slowly she walked around
the garden. She saw something move around the
bush. 'Surprise,' said her mother. 'Happy Easter
too.'

Chloe Maspero (7)
Locking Primary School, Weston-super-Mare

Untitled

Mum walked into the house. She opened the
front room door but no one was there. She
opened the kitchen door. 'Surprise!' said Sally and
Dad. 'Happy Mother's Day.'
'Wow thank you,' said Mum. 'That was a great
surprise. Some day can you do it again?'
'OK,' said Dad and Sally.

Amber Panesar (7)
Locking Primary School, Weston-super-Mare

When I Met A Fairy

One night I found fairies in my room and they were beautiful. They turned me into a fairy and took me to a magical place. They called it Fairyland. When I was there I met a fairy king and queen. Suddenly I was myself again. Oh goodnight!

Ella Judge (9)

Locking Primary School, Weston-super-Mare

Untitled

It was a windy day. That day we had an earthquake. I wished I had clean water and proper food. I was in Haiti wanting my parents to come back to life but my wish was just not coming true. I had to hunt for my food.

Tyran Burnley (8)
Locking Primary School, Weston-super-Mare

The Fairytale Garden

Lucy was walking to school and she noticed a
secret path. She walked down it and was amazed
when she saw a fairytale garden. It was beautiful.
It led her to school but nobody believed her
when she told them of her journey. The next day
the path was gone.

Megan Reed (8)
Locking Primary School, Weston-super-Mare

The Ice Cream Van

Sophie was going shopping with her friends. As they were walking down the high street she heard haunting music coming towards her. She panicked, she was shaky and scared.
Then a bright colourful van came over. 'Two ice creams for £2!' said a jolly voice. Sophie was so embarrassed.

Leila Deeley (10)
Manor House School, Leatherhead

Gus The Clever Puppy

'Gus! Where are you?' Louise shouted loudly for her puppy. There was no reply. Suddenly she heard a thump. It was Gus! In his mouth he was carrying a huge, juicy bone covered in mud. Gus had sniffed out the bone in the rose garden and wrecked it! 'Oh no!'

Elizabeth Ahn (10)

Manor House School, Leatherhead

Alone

Bella came into the driveway at midnight, exhausted from the party. Everything was black and quiet. Too quiet! Suddenly she saw a face in the window. Not her Mum's or her Dad's. Bella looked again, it was gone. She was terrified. Was she really all alone?

Julia Drake (10)
Manor House School, Leatherhead

Vampire Night

Janie put on her most beautiful dress for the party. She tied up her hair, put her lip gloss on and got in the car. When she arrived she pushed the doors open and came face to face with vampires! 'It is supposed to be a vampire party,' she heard.

Dalia Al-Dujaili (10)
Manor House School, Leatherhead

A Big Surprise For Jemma

One beautiful sunny day when Jemma got home from school, she was expecting her mum and dad to be home. They had promised that they would all go out to dinner for her 11th birthday. But when Jemma opened the playroom door everyone inside shouted out, 'Happy birthday Jemma!'

Ruby Lamborn (10)
Manor House School, Leatherhead

The Pixie

Kelly woke up, there was someone at the door. She was home alone so she didn't know if she should answer it. She made up her mind, she opened it and standing there was a pixie with a pointy nose. Suddenly, Kelly woke up. It was all a dream!

Tara Wood (11)

Manor House School, Leatherhead

Granny's Day Out With Me

It's Granny's day out with me. She always takes me somewhere boring like to the park, but today she said she'd take me somewhere really cool! She took me to a different park! I can't count on Granny for fun days out, but I wouldn't change her one bit.

Florence McCulloch (10)

Manor House School, Leatherhead

A Twisted Tale

Sarah opened her mouth in despair as the castle tumbled down. The bright orange flames were licking away at the final wall. She backed away, cautious as a cat. She shed a tear and watched her gown turn black. Then she turned her head, only to hear the words … 'Cut!'

Georgia Proctor (11)
Manor House School, Leatherhead

The Seven Dwarfs And Their New Friend

'High ho, high ho,' sang the dwarfs on their way back home. Once they got there they found that everything was locked. Suddenly a loud thundering snore came from inside. So they climbed on each other's shoulders and peered through the bedroom window. Lying on their beds was Goldilocks.

Thea Grieve (11)

Manor House School, Leatherhead

The Killer Fairy

My mobile phone rang and I looked everywhere.
It was nowhere to be seen. I went into the
kitchen; my eyes were drawn to the washing
machine where my phone was going around in
circles. By the time I got it out it had been killed
by the Fairy Liquid.

Bethany Fielding (10)
Manor House School, Leatherhead

The Birthday Confusion

Joe wondered where his parents were. He was
on a holiday and it was his birthday. So he decided
to go and find his family. He got to the lobby
and noticed that it was decorated for a party.
Excitedly Joe looked at the banner and read,
'Happy birthday Patrick!'

Jennifer Hobbs (10)
Manor House School, Leatherhead

A Tale Of The Unexpected

I looked up at the great monument. Fools, believing the myths and legends! They didn't scare me. 'Would you like to take my photo?' pleaded my sister. Holding the camera up to my face, I saw a ghostly figure staring down. I froze! When I looked again the pale child had vanished.

Sophie Smith (11)

Manor House School, Leatherhead

Pingu's Outing

One afternoon Pingu was out fishing with his dad. Pingu's line gave a sharp tug. 'I've caught a fish,' cried Pingu excitedly. His flippers strained at the effort, keeping the rod above the water. He slid along the ice, fell into the cold water and the plasticine penguin sank.

Martha Pratt (11)

Manor House School, Leatherhead

The Ending Story Of Red Riding Hood

Once upon a time a little girl had to go and see
her grandmother who was seriously ill. Her name
was Little Red Riding Hood. On the way she
met a mean fox, he pretended to be friendly but
instead ate Red Riding Hood all up! Oh what a
shame!

Nadine Reeves (10)

Manor House School, Leatherhead

The Revenge Of The Fire Mice

Black smoke appeared from the fireplace and
millions of walking fireballs stomped across
the carpet towards a cat. The leader, Minimus,
sizzled the cat's hairs on his tail. Then he shouted,
'Charge!' and they all ran to the cat, and they too
sizzled his tail and sent him packing angrily.

Henrietta Mills (11)
Manor House School, Leatherhead

Henry's Dilemma

One day Henry found a hole in his watering can.
He spoke to his wife Lisa about it. She suggested
that he should weld it. Henry got some metal, lit a
fire. 'Quick we'll need some water to put it out.'
'But there's a hole in my watering can Lisa.'

Amy Norman (10)
Manor House School, Leatherhead

Menisha Mermaid's Tail

Menisha's sparkling forget-me-not blue eyes gleamed with excitement as she plunged into the cool water. She thought her feet had turned into miniature ice blocks. She felt the churning water moving around her waist. She pondered staying there forever. She could as she was a mermaid.

Katherine Mayhew (10)
Manor House School, Leatherhead

The Three Little Pigs ...
With A Twist

And he huffed and he puffed and blew the little house down. The two pigs ran to find their brother's brick house. Unfortunately this was Georgian times and the third little pig had bricked up his doors and windows to avoid the window tax. So the two pigs were eaten.

Emily Hutchins (10)
Manor House School, Leatherhead

79

Dead Living

I opened the dusty door with a creak. It was dark
and deserted. Why did they want me here on
my birthday? 'Surprise!' a voice drooled from the
corner. The light flickered on. I stepped back with
surprise. It was Charlie, an old school friend. But
he died last Christmas!

Natasha Jones (10)

Manor House School, Leatherhead

The Tooth Fairy

I flew into my mushroom-shaped house. The lights were on and the curtains were drawn. I realised that the children's teeth I'd taken from their pillows were gone. I flew up and down the stairs, I couldn't find them anywhere. Now how would I make the magic fairy dust?

Jade Dipré (10)
Manor House School, Leatherhead

Hissing Snake

What's that hissing? It's a snake, thought Daniel.
I'm scared. Daniel climbed a tree. *I shall wait here
for the snake to go.*
Later, when the hissing stopped, he came down.
When he looked at his bike, the tyre was flat, so
that's what was hissing. There wasn't a snake!

Daniel Hill (10)

Motcombe CE (VA) Primary School, Shaftesbury

The Surprise Sweets

'I've got to go out now!' shouted Mum. She slammed the door. The babysitter arrived at seven. I was wandering down the hall, when suddenly the hall door burst open! 'Surprise!' beamed my sister. She was holding a huge secret stash of sweets.

'Wow,' I beamed, 'That's loads of sweets!'

Toby Rose (10)
Motcombe CE (VA) Primary School, Shaftesbury

Honours!

I entered room 10 shaking! The elderly, sinister man sitting in the corner reminded me that I didn't want to visit this place again. 'Begin,' he said crossly. I played better than ever before. The audience went wild with applause. The man changed suddenly and said, 'Honours!' 'Fantastic!' I replied.

Lauren Hayes (10)
Motcombe CE (VA) Primary School, Shaftesbury

The Stranger

Suddenly the curtains flapped and outside I saw
a dark figure walk across the garden. I froze,
was it a ghost? I wasn't sure. Then the stranger
disappeared. Then I heard the front door open.
I went downstairs and I saw Gran holding
Whiskers. I thought she was the ghost!

Georgina Cluett (9)
Motcombe CE (VA) Primary School, Shaftesbury

Missing!

One day, at about 2pm we went to the park,
Rupert and Monty went missing! 'Rupert, Monty?'
I shouted. But no reply. I ran home to tell Mum.
So we went back to the park and they were
there. 'But you weren't there a minute ago,' I
mumbled.

Albany Milton (9)

Motcombe CE (VA) Primary School, Shaftesbury

The New Neighbours

One day there was a house over the road for sale. Someone wanted to move in. So they did. The neighbours were very nice. They gave all the other neighbours sweets and treats. They all were very happy about where they lived. They had a big moving in party.

Emily Williams (10)

Motcombe CE (VA) Primary School, Shaftesbury

The Three Clever Mice

One day three mice were trying to get to the cheese. They built a bridge out of rulers. They were halfway across when the cat stopped them. 'I'm going to eat you,' said the cat. 'No you're not, there's a ball of wool.' And they ran to the cheese.

Nathan Upshall (10)
Motcombe CE (VA) Primary School, Shaftesbury

Untitled

It was the middle of the night and Anna heard something suspicious coming from above her room, it was like a howling sound and it was scratching the ground. Anna was very scared. She went up the stairs to find her little cat. 'Mittens! How did you get up here?'

Liah Wright (10)
Motcombe CE (VA) Primary School, Shaftesbury

Forest Adventure

Lucy and Jess went into the forest. They stayed in a cottage. 'Don't go near the wolves!' Dad said. They saw the pack and stupidly followed. The wolves stopped, turned and started to chase the girls. Luckily, as they were ready to pounce, a hunter appeared and shot them dead!

Lucy Cuff (11)

Motcombe CE (VA) Primary School, Shaftesbury

Come Quick

'Come quick! A cat just ran out of the house and
we've left the rat cage open!' We dashed inside
to the study, stared at the cage, only one rat was
visible. We searched every nook and cranny.
Double checked the cage to find she was curled
up in her house!

Morganne Cannon-Langford (10)
Motcombe CE (VA) Primary School, Shaftesbury

Nobody Remembered My Birthday!

The house was empty. *I cannot believe Mum and Dad have forgotten my birthday!* I thought to myself. I heard footsteps but nobody was there. 'Surprise!' all my friends and family screeched. I screamed my head off! (not literally of course). What a great surprise birthday party, it was amazing!

Katie Hockett (10)

Motcombe CE (VA) Primary School, Shaftesbury

The Chop!

Anne Boleyn was waiting in the terrifying tower. It was dark and cold but she felt nothing. The day came; light shone. She walked serenely to her fate. There was no going back. History was in the making. Calmly she rested her fragile neck on the bloodstained block. *Chop!*

Alicia Fitzgerald (10)
Motcombe CE (VA) Primary School, Shaftesbury

Bjorn The Viking Who Could Not Remember

Bjorn was always forgetting. He was clumsy and never remembered much. Then the fearsome Pichu army came to raid the village. Weapons were prohibited here, and only the chief knew where they were kept. But so did Bjorn, who found the weapons and defeated the enemy with some cunning ambushes.

Jack Banister (11)

Motcombe CE (VA) Primary School, Shaftesbury

Wow Boys And Girls

Yo boys and girls, yo boys and girls. The donkeys
and the cymbals just hip hopped onto Jupiter.
The rest of the safari park just went crazy mad.
Hippos are jumping, all going mad. Plates are
spinning, spoons are rattling, forks playing cards.
Such fun the planets can have.

Keanna Richens (11)
Motcombe CE (VA) Primary School, Shaftesbury

The Mad Zoo

My mum and I went to the zoo on a nice sunny day. But when we got there the monkeys were throwing bananas, the birds were squawking, the lions were loose, the snakes had eaten a boy. The zoo was so mad that Mum and I ran off home!

Jordan Anstey (11)
Motcombe CE (VA) Primary School, Shaftesbury

Scrambled Egg

I'm here at the scene of a serious accident, involving an unusual egg character. In the last few moments his identity has been revealed as local legend Humpty-Dumpty. The king's men and their horses are working hard to put him back together again. Olivia Matthews reporting for nursery news.

Olivia Matthews (10)

Motcombe CE (VA) Primary School, Shaftesbury

Old Duke Of York

A long time ago, in the walled town of York, there lived a grand old duke. He was extremely powerful and led an army of ten thousand soldiers. Every day he marched his regiment of men to the top of a nearby high hill and marched them back down again!

Maisie Chalk (10)

Motcombe CE (VA) Primary School, Shaftesbury

Untitled

At night, all silent. Creaky floorboards squeaked.
The sound of the telly echoed around the room.
Stuff went bump in the attic. *Thump, thump* went
the cupboard door. Suddenly Abbey (my big
sister) jumped out of my cupboard. 'Hello my
friend,' she shrieked.
'Abbey, stop it.'
'Sorry,' said Abbey.

Sam Starr (10)
Motcombe CE (VA) Primary School, Shaftesbury

Awake

One stormy day, James was rushed into hospital because he needed a heart transplant. The second he woke up in hospital, he was in the operation room. The operation was to give him another heart instead of his old one. The working heart was donated by a very loving charity.

Billie-Jayne Addis (9)
Newport Community Primary School, Barnstaple

Untitled

There once was a mansion where some rich people lived. They died five years ago, kids normally went inside there. It was also deserted. Most people went in there and never came out because a ghost haunted in there, searching for its gold ...

Ryan Fell (10)
Oughton Primary & Nursery School, Hitchin

The Pixies

One early morning, in Pixie Hollow, the rainbow fairies were getting ready to do their big rainbow of the year. The garden fairies were making dresses out of big green leaves. They were getting ready for the big parade. When the parade was over they went home to relax.

Leoni Perry (9)
Oughton Primary & Nursery School, Hitchin

Baa Baa Pink Sheep

Baa, baa pink sheep have you any candy? Yes mam, yes mam but it's very sandy. Don't get it for your mother, don't get it for your father and don't even think about giving it to your baby brother. If it's very sandy he won't like candy, sadly.

Deanna Simms (9)
Oughton Primary & Nursery School, Hitchin

Spooky Ways!

In a crooked house, an old man was sitting down watching television. He left the door open and in walked an intruder. He took a knife out and turned invisible. It was a ghost. No one knows what happened to the old man.

Rhiannon Pateman (9)
Oughton Primary & Nursery School, Hitchin

Ghost

The cupboard had been making strange noises for one week. Everyone had been too scared to open it. Out of nowhere I ran downstairs and pulled it open. Out came a bright ghost. It opened the front door, ran down the street and never came back again. Hooray!

Amy McInally (11)
Oughton Primary & Nursery School, Hitchin

My Best Friend Benjie

I was waiting patiently, worrying if he was going to come. Then all of a sudden, out of nowhere, I saw his shimmering fin skimming through the water! Benjie, my best friend, an amazing dolphin! He's spectacular in all his shows, and his performances shine just like his infectious smile.

Chloe Lockwood (11)

Oughton Primary & Nursery School, Hitchin

The Mad Scientist And The Roller Coaster

The mad scientist was bored. He'd invented a roller coaster. Because he was mad, he put the wrong screws in and no brakes. People waited for a ride at the fair. It was great fun until the coaster broke free from the tracks! It travelled bumpily across the entire town …

Abby Ladyman (10)
Oughton Primary & Nursery School, Hitchin

Secluded Island Of Treasure!

On a secluded island, Suzie and Mark stared in
shock. 'What can we do with it?' exclaimed Mark.
Suzie did not answer. Suddenly she dashed off in a
rush! Mark just followed.
Six hours later they were buried in gold.
Glistening rubies blinded Mark's eyes, he fell to
the ground!

Maisie Cooper (11)
Oughton Primary & Nursery School, Hitchin

Untitled

Jack and Jill ran up the hill. Both were out of puff.
Jill's legs were sore. She couldn't run anymore. So
Jack went off in a huff.

Sean Robertson (9)
Oughton Primary & Nursery School, Hitchin

The Evil Dog

Once upon a time, there was a spooky castle with an evil dog. If anyone went near it, they would run. One day someone went there. The dog was asleep. He crept in. Someone saw him and kicked him out. He was never seen again.

Shanika Gibbins (9)

Oughton Primary & Nursery School, Hitchin

A Girl Who Was Always Bullied

Rowde School was the happiest school in the world. However there was a girl who always got bullied by a group of girls. They always called her names and pushed her. So she talked to Mr Ball and he sorted it all out and they became best friends forever.

Jasmine Reader (8)
Rowde CE (VA) Primary School, Devizes

Surprise Birthday

A girl walked into the house, no one was there.
She walked over the bridge and when she was
walking, a brick fell but she got to the other side.
'Happy birthday.'
She walked back over but fell in the water.
'Let's go to Pizza Hut!'

Phoebe Wills (7)
Rowde CE (VA) Primary School, Devizes

Hairy Billy

Alex woke up with a fright. Something was clambering down the chimney. *Crash!* It landed with a thud. When it got up Alex murmured, 'Who are you and why are you so hairy?' Alex saw the shadow moving towards him and then ... 'Surprise - happy birthday, Son.'

Daniel Taylor (8)
Rowde CE (VA) Primary School, Devizes

Missing Kids

On Mother's Day a mum woke up to find her children were missing. She looked in the house, the garden and the park. However, they were not there!

It turned out that they were with their dad, buying chocolates. 'Happy Mother's Day,' they shouted and ate the chocolates.

Katie Miller (8)
Rowde CE (VA) Primary School, Devizes

Good Night

Sally was fast asleep - then she heard *boom, boom!*
It was coming from her door. 'Who is it?' There
was no reply, then the door opened wide. Sally
screamed, 'Help, help, help.' She could see two
people! It was her mum and dad coming to give
her a big hug.

Wednesday Gilbert (8)
Rowde CE (VA) Primary School, Devizes

Easter Surprise

Megan woke up in the middle of the night with a fright. Then she heard a turning sound so she clambered downstairs and saw a trail of Easter eggs. She followed them.
Later the trail stopped. Then she looked straight at a head.

Charlie Duncan (8)
Rowde CE (VA) Primary School, Devizes

The Terrible Teacher

There was a lovely teacher and she wore lots of
dresses.
One day she turned into a terrible teacher who
had big fangs with blood. The children ran to the
headmaster screaming!
'What is the matter?'
'Terrible teacher!'

Bliss Sibley Greenslade (7)
Rowde CE (VA) Primary School, Devizes

Humpty-Dumpty

Humpty-Dumpty always liked to sit on the wall.
Suddenly he fell off, so he called the army but
they could not fix him. They had not had any
breakfast, so they had scrambled egg.

Robyn Johnson (7)
Rowde CE (VA) Primary School, Devizes

The Stupid Crocodile
Who Never Brushed His Teeth

Mr Billy drank fizzy drinks and never brushed his
teeth.
One day a mouse came along. 'You must brush
your teeth!'
Next came Mrs Mousse and said, 'You can't eat
me!'
'Yes I can.' He leapt onto her back … *chop* - and
then his teeth were gone. What a ninny!

Mitchel Wilson (8)
Rowde CE (VA) Primary School, Devizes

Josh And The Zombie

Once there was a boy called Josh. Behind him was a one-legged zombie. Josh killed the zombie and ran home. He said, 'Mum let me in!' Then he killed his mum and said, 'Ha-ha, Lady!'

Thomas Bailey (8)
Rowde CE (VA) Primary School, Devizes

Humpty

Humpty was sat on a wall - as he got down, *crash*, he broke into one million pieces. When the scary king found out, he yelled to his brave army, 'Right this will be our breakfast.'
After that the king and his army had enough breakfast to last forever.

Maddy Parker (8)
Rowde CE (VA) Primary School, Devizes

The Dog In The Snow

There was a dog happily playing in the snow.
He saw some giant footsteps. They led him in a
circle. However, he realised it was his own paws
and ended up chasing his tail.

Mae Wells (8)
Rowde CE (VA) Primary School, Devizes

Dragon

Jen lived in China. It was the year of the dragon.
She was eating breakfast and heard a knock at her
door.
Each day the dragon came until he said, 'Hello,
I am your dad. It's the year of the dragon
remember?'

Abigail Baker (8)
Rowde CE (VA) Primary School, Devizes

What Happens When You Wake Up In The Middle Of The Night?

An army officer heard some noises. He went looking for the leader's cabin. He opened a door and looked at the angry faces. 'The enemy!' he screamed and ran and tripped over a teddy bear singing 'Twinkle, Twinkle Little Star'.

Holly Baker (8)
Rowde CE (VA) Primary School, Devizes

The Ghost On The Staircase

Genny saw a ghost. She got a net. She went back.
The ghost wasn't there.
Five years later she saw the ghost. She caught it.
She gave it to the museum. The museum put it in
a ghost cage for people to see. Now you know
ghosts exist.

Catherine Gray (7)
Rowde CE (VA) Primary School, Devizes

The Dragon

A girl once got ready to go to school. Then she went to get some breakfast. Then there was a knock at the door. It was a dragon. He said, 'Hi.' Then he said, 'Bye.'

Esme Sibley Greenslade (7)
Rowde CE (VA) Primary School, Devizes

School Trip

Daisy was on a school trip. She fell over and grazed her knee. Daisy went to see some cows. She had to be careful because there were bulls. She went to see ducks in the lake swimming. Later in the day, she had to go on the coach home.

Genevieve Bennett (8)
Rowde CE (VA) Primary School, Devizes

Under The Ocean

Sam and his friends went on a boat, going diving.
They jumped in, they swam and swam and saw a
monster. It had lots of tentacles. It was a jellyfish.
They swam away and quickly went to the boat
and told their mum about it.

William Plank (8)
Rowde CE (VA) Primary School, Devizes

Midnight Surprise

One night, at midnight, when no one was awake,
a ghost got everybody up with a shock. It tried to
haunt a girl with a bomb. However it was just her
mum in the end.

Ethan Bailey (7)
Rowde CE (VA) Primary School, Devizes

Sam Got On A Wall

Sam sat on a wall. Sam had a fall. All of the king's horses said, 'Tea is on me!' They said, 'We will have him for tea. First we have to cook him then eat him.'

Ellie Jay Alnwick (8)
Rowde CE (VA) Primary School, Devizes

Ben's Big Shock

Ben woke up with a pound. 'Ah!' he said. He went
to the cupboard and clambered through the mess
to get clothes. Just then a brush came down.
'Wah!' Ben screamed. Then some soot came
down.
'Sorry mate,' the chimney sweep said.

Joshua Roach (7)
Rowde CE (VA) Primary School, Devizes

The Party

Katy was invited to a party. She met a prince
called George. After that she went home.
Then the prince said, 'Is this your shoe?'
Katy replied, 'Yes it is.'
George said, 'Will you marry me?'

Zara Hues (8)
Rowde CE (VA) Primary School, Devizes

The Box

Amy woke up. She found herself in an omen box. 'Where am I?' she said. The box creaked and the door opened. Amy stepped out. 'I remember this place.'
'The water park!' shouted her family.
'Whoo-hoo. Let's play,' shouted Amy excitedly.

Emma Horney (7)
Rowde CE (VA) Primary School, Devizes

Ghostly Goings-On

Softly, he approached the old ravaged door. Jack outstretched his arms to touch the green slime oozing down the door. His fingers wrapped around the cold iron handle and opened it. There, behind the door, was a ghostly figure covered in slime. Jack screamed and ran out of the house.

Frazier Perry (11)
St Andrew's CE Primary School, Sherborne

The Missing Alpacas

It was 10am. Henry was late feeding the alpacas.
When he got to the field, to his horror, they were
gone and the gate was wide open! He ran all the
way home. 'The alpacas are gone,' explained
Henry frantically.
'Ha-ha, yes, gone to be shorn,' said Mum.
'Phew!'

Henry Ward (11)
St Andrew's CE Primary School, Sherborne

135

Jack And Jill

Jack and Jill struggled to climb up the tall mountain to get a barrel of strong cider. Jack drank all the cider and got very drunk. Then suddenly fell drunkenly up the tall mountain. Jill got drunk and fell behind Jack and cracked her crown and broke her big knee.

Elliott Morton (10)
St Andrew's CE Primary School, Sherborne

Emma's Tragedy

When Emma got to school, she remembered it
was non school uniform day. 'Oh no!' she said
with a shocked voice.
Someone tapped her on the shoulder and said,
'Are you alright Emma?'
'I've forgotten that it's non-uniform today, haven't
I?'
'No silly, that's tomorrow,' came the saving
words.

Georgina Williamson (11)
St Andrew's CE Primary School, Sherborne

Do Not Worry

Jane woke up early in the morning. The house was quiet and untouched. Everything was exactly the same as it was last night. Jane crept into her mum and dad's room, but nobody was there. Jane found a note lying crumpled on the table, it read 'Do not worry'.

Annie Brignall (10)
St Andrew's CE Primary School, Sherborne

In The Trench

Dong! A bullet skimmed his head. Pleads of men, long since gone, echoed about. Hissing eerie mist floated effortlessly through the stream-like trench. The end was near. The enemy came closer. Silence, gunfire ceased. Fingers clenched, blisters throbbing. Just need two more shots then … out of ammo! Game over.

Andrew Priest (10)
St Andrew's CE Primary School, Sherborne

The Princess And The Guinea Pig

The beautiful princess went to kiss the cute, furry guinea pig, in the hope she would have a dashing prince to marry. When she kissed the guinea pig it turned into a huge, snarling lion with extremely sharp claws and fangs. The princess turned around and ran for her life!

Aimee-Lauren Gillman (10)
St Andrew's CE Primary School, Sherborne

Silly Hamster

I came home from school one evening and saw
my parents (as always). Then I went to bed. I saw
a shadow up my stairs. I thought it could be my
mum and dad but it had sharp teeth and red eyes.
However, it was just my hamster, Stuart.

Ethan Willett (9)
St Cleer Primary School, Liskeard

Monster Tale

I crept downstairs and saw a flash. I went into the
silent kitchen. I suddenly saw a monster, so I ran
towards it being brave. It ran outside, so I chased
it down the street. It disappeared into thin air!
Was my mind playing funny tricks on me?

Sam Wiltshire (9)

St Cleer Primary School, Liskeard

142

The Killer

One misty morning down at Pearl Harbour, 1941,
a German bomber dropped a nuclear bomb that
set fire to all of the warships and all of the people
died that were near. So the British sent as many
bombers and Spitfires to shoot down all of the
German bombers.

Fletcher Mason (9)
St Cleer Primary School, Liskeard

143

The Garden

I love going to my granny's house because you get lost there. Well it is so huge! I love the gorgeous smells in the garden. The colours dazzle me. Every time I go there I am stunned! The flowers take me into another world. Have you felt like this before?

Grace Emma Smart (10)
St Cleer Primary School, Liskeard

The Roaring Sound

As I crept into the gloomy kitchen, I heard a
roaring sound in the old and haunted living room.
As I got my foam sword, I tripped over Dad's
slippers. *Bang!* I fell into the washing basket! I
switched the light on but the roaring sound was
the TV.

Leila Sprague (9)
St Cleer Primary School, Liskeard

145

Ghost

I came home one day. It was all black. Suddenly the lights turned on and off. I was very scared. It must be a ghost. So I went to Argos to get some ghost busting gear.
When I got home I found out it was my little brother. How annoying.

Tristan Bolton (10)
St Cleer Primary School, Liskeard

Was It Really Harry?

I went downstairs to see what the racket was all about. It was only my pet hamster, Harry. So I went back to bed. Surely he couldn't make that much noise. His mouth is only 1cm long. I just forgot all about it. I was able to forget!

Jacob Pethick (8)
St Cleer Primary School, Liskeard

Dragon

When I was 10, I had a magic dragon. It was
a sprite dragon, I loved it so much but it was
just a baby and it grew and grew so I had to do
something. My dad had a field and I let him free.
He's happy now. Hooray!

Beith Fenlon (10)
St Cleer Primary School, Liskeard

The Fright At School

Bell was walking home from St Cleer school. She crossed the road, ran up the path until she reached the spooky church. She went on the bank to catch her breath. 'What is that?' screamed Bell in a panic. She ran home. She was afraid of the deathly, unknown silence!

Isabel Cliffe (10)

St Cleer Primary School, Liskeard

My Nightmare

One horrible day I went to my nightmare … the dentist. When we arrived I was shaking forever. When I went in he looked in my mouth. He took one look and said, 'Your teeth are fine.'

Selina Payne (11)
St John's Walworth CE Primary School, London

Untitled

The room was deadly silent until I heard a creak by the door. I quickly sprung out of my bed to see. Until the door opened and it was my mum bringing my lovely warm, hot chocolate in a Noddy mug.

James Kamara (11)
St John's Walworth CE Primary School, London

Untitled

I walked into a cloud of fog all alone, wondering where I could be. I was shaking. I was also very scared. The fog started clearing away. I then saw my house door. I slowly took out my keys and opened the door and - 'Surprise! Happy birthday!'

Ebony Niles (11)
St John's Walworth CE Primary School, London

Untitled

In a town where they only ate sardines, was Tom, who wanted to be a scientist. He wanted to make a machine that would make different food. People became so greedy that the machine broke and came to an end. Back to sardines for them.

Deborah Adereep (11)
St John's Walworth CE Primary School, London

The Dark, Dark Night

It was a scary night in the house and his bedroom was full of scary pictures. He was walking around the living room. Abel was all alone and waiting for his parents. But then he looked behind the sofa and his parents screamed out, 'Go to bed!'

Abel Tewdros (11)

St John's Walworth CE Primary School, London

Scared

As I entered the school fearfully, nobody was there. I shouted, 'Is anybody there?' All I heard was the echoing of my voice. I started to lose my temper, I turned and then … *Bang! Bang!* The door closed shut. Trapped and nowhere to escape.

Abu Bangura (11)
St John's Walworth CE Primary School, London

The Race

I put my feet on the starting blocks and tensed. I was against the fastest boy in the school - Alex Smith. The starting gun went and I ran. I was behind, but I was in front in seconds and before I knew it, I had won!

Jonathan Linkens (11)

St John's Walworth CE Primary School, London

Lights Off

The time had come, all the lights were off. There
was a noise coming from the schoolyard. I went
in to investigate. There was a family of foxes, I
was trembling like mad. Soon to find out, it was
children in costumes.

Yetunde Akiode (11)
St John's Walworth CE Primary School, London

Snow

The road was deserted. The street was quiet.
All I knew, it was snowing. Soft white snow lay
calmly on the ground, freshly laid out. The snow
as so marvellous until … dramatically everybody
rushed out of doors and disturbed the delightful
snow. I was so heartbroken.

Kemi Ayoola (11)
St John's Walworth CE Primary School, London

Surprise

I saw a snowflake fall on my hand. At first I didn't know what it was and then more came down. Then I knew what it was. It was snowing. What a lovely surprise on the day it was my birthday. I got a big, big, big surprise.

Lauren Rowe (10)
St John's Walworth CE Primary School, London

Jerry In The Dark

In the dark and gloomy night, Jerry heard something downstairs. When he got downstairs, he grabbed a pan and looked in the fridge, which was half open. He turned on the light. It was Dad with his finger in an ice cream tub.

Tremont Deigh (11)
St John's Walworth CE Primary School, London

Death?

As Marice entered the garden, her face fell in
depressing shock. Lying on the desolate grass,
was her mother, surrounded by a swarm of
weeping family members.
Later, Marice held her funeral, continuously
weeping her eyes out! As Marice paid her tribute,
her mother sprung from the coffin.
'She's alive!'

Elizabeth Agbonjinmi (11)
St John's Walworth CE Primary School, London

The Night I Became A Vampire

Night-time; the time when the vampires come out.
I collapsed at first when I saw one. I woke up as a vampire, with sharp canines and the habit of biting people and sucking their blood. I now need to reveal to the world: I'm a vampire.

Azyra Williams (11)
St John's Walworth CE Primary School, London

Untitled

Kye was looking for his friend in a dark alley.
He saw something lurking in the dark. Kye was
terrified and the creature ran rapidly towards him
and said, 'Hello mate.' It was Tod, looking for him.

Joshua Plummer (11)
St John's Walworth CE Primary School, London

Spooky!

My heart was beating as fast as a cheetah and then I put one foot on the step and it made a loud creak. Some huge eyes came flying at me and I was petrified. I then found out it was the next-door neighbour's cat.

Harry Vickers (11)
St John's Walworth CE Primary School, London

Untitled

The gigantic spooky house was filled with
cobwebs and dirty skeletons. Suddenly a spider
was creeping out from the window. I was very
scared but the door was creaking.
'Surprise!'
Wow, what a Christmas party.

Brooke Ferede (11)
St John's Walworth CE Primary School, London

Break Time

As I was playing, a gigantic mountain came out of the ground. A goat was on the top. I went up the mountain to see if the goat was OK. Then, at that moment, the goat did a leap and I fell off the mountain onto a big mattress.

Thomas Crisp (11)
St Lawrence CE (A) Primary School, Chobham

What's In Your Bedroom?

What's in your bedroom? Does anyone know? Is
it a dog scratching its nose or a pig eating a fig?
Maybe a cat breaking your bat? The only way to
find out is to have a look about.
I went through the white door.
Guess what I saw … ?

Holly Duffield (11)
St Lawrence CE (A) Primary School, Chobham

The Halloween Night

It was Halloween night, everyone was dressed up. I dressed up as a werewolf. We were having a party in a house that apparently was haunted. Everyone was gone and I was tidying up. Then I heard a noise. Then I looked, phew it was just the ceiling leaking!

Terry Riedel (10)

St Lawrence CE (A) Primary School, Chobham

What's In Your Cupboard?

I lay in bed one night wondering about tomorrow.
Suddenly, something creaked, it was coming from
the cupboard. What was it … ? I slowly crept
out of bed and paused for a second, then moved
towards the cupboard. I opened it … It was only
a dodgy coat hanger from Morrisons!

Reece McCarthy (10)
St Lawrence CE (A) Primary School, Chobham

I Know Someone Is There

The doorbell rang … I slowly walked to it. I opened it halfway. I squeezed my eyes as tight as I could and opened it all the way. All there was, was a light winking at me. As I stood, my mum said, 'Hello,' and walked in.

Elena Rico (10)
St Lawrence CE (A) Primary School, Chobham

Out In My Garden

When I stepped out, I started to dribble. The trees were lollipops, the flowers were white and brown chocolate. The water in the pond looked like a milkshake. The stones around it were big balls of ice cream and the fish were chewing gum … !
'Wake up!' said Mum.

Emily Randall (10)
St Lawrence CE (A) Primary School, Chobham

Getting Up

Oh! Not school again! Why, why, why?
'Come on, get up!' Mum says.
I bury my head and ignore! Well the school
meals are pretty nice. I sling myself out of bed
and straight downstairs for my heaven-like Coco
Pops! That's why I like mornings.

Keaton Kavanagh (11)
St Lawrence CE (A) Primary School, Chobham

Bedtime Blues

Time passed … It was nearly my bedtime. I was sitting in the lounge watching TV. My mum was warmed up in a blanket, so was my brother. My dad was playing darts, and I sat there with my feet up, watching Mr Bean. This is how my bedtime was! Night.

Rachel Lee (11)

St Lawrence CE (A) Primary School, Chobham

What's In Your Cupboard?

What's in your cupboard? Nobody knows. Is it a mouse biting his toes or a cat eating its food? Maybe it's a skunk eating my junk? Is it a dog eating a hedgehog or is it a bear having a pear? I know what it is, it's a toad.

David Wiltshire (10)

St Lawrence CE (A) Primary School, Chobham

Monstrous Teddies

It was a Halloween night. People trick or treating,
but I was at home, not knowing what to do.
There was a creak from my wardrobe. Nothing
was there. I lay back down. My drawer was
banging this time. A monster jumped out at me.
Huh! It was a teddy!

George Williams (10)
St Lawrence CE (A) Primary School, Chobham

The Open Door

Ding-dong! Edward opened the door. No one was there. He walked back to the kitchen. He walked up the stairs and saw his mum and dad. 'So it was you who opened the door?'
'No!' shouted his parents, scared.
'Then who was it?'

Charlie Craig (9)
Shamblehurst Primary School, Southampton

No Presents!

It was Christmas Day and Luke rushed downstairs to unwrap his presents. Suddenly a horrific sight met his eyes, there were no presents. Luke panicked. It was Christmas Day and there were no presents! Luke ran to his mum and dad's room to see all the presents right there!

Daniel Walford (9)

Shamblehurst Primary School, Southampton

The Boy Who Knew Everything Or Did He?

A hundred years in the future, there was an extremely intelligent boy of fifteen. He knew everything about everything. There was nowhere he hadn't been. He even knew how to become invisible in 8.5 seconds! There was no word he couldn't understand. He, couldn't be dumb!

James Cushing (9)

Shamblehurst Primary School, Southampton

Hiking Horror!

'Bye Mum,' said Fred one boiling summer day.
Fred was strolling to his aunt Selma's house. His
aunt's house was high in the misty peaks.
He was hiking along when he heard leaves
rustling. He had the feeling someone was
watching him. He carried on and was grabbed.
'Auntie!'

Samuel Adams (8)
Shamblehurst Primary School, Southampton

Untitled

'Let's go to the cinema,' said Lisa excitedly.
'OK, let's go!'
'What shall we watch?' said Rachael, surprisingly.
'Let's watch The Princess and the Frog,' shouted
Lisa.
So they got in the car. Lisa got out of the car and
Lisa slipped up. 'Can we go home now?'

Rachael Phillips (9)
Shamblehurst Primary School, Southampton

Empty Ghost

Scott came home from school. 'Mum, Dad, I'm home.' There was no one there. Scott went upstairs. There was no one there. Suddenly, there was a loud *bang!* 'Who's there?' He got out of bed and opened the door. There was a ghost. Scott ran downstairs and left.

Scott Purchase (9)
Shamblehurst Primary School, Southampton

A Mystery That Wasn't

Crazy Chloe went to the zoo. Chloe's favourite
animal was a spotty cheetah. The cheetahs are
just a bit beyond the entrance. Chloe ran super
fast but they weren't there. 'Where are they?'
'They are just being fed. Come and help me!'
'Oww!' cried Chloe.
'They don't hurt.'

Chloe Netherwood (9)
Shamblehurst Primary School, Southampton

Vampires

Suddenly I heard footsteps coming from downstairs. I went to look what it was, but when I went to look I saw twenty vampires. I was thinking, *should I make a run for it?*
One of the vampires said, 'Get her and eat her!'
Then I got eaten. Yum!

Eloise Hanslip (8)
Shamblehurst Primary School, Southampton

The Alien

An alien was stranded on Mars and all he wanted was a hot dog. He had no money and no matter what he did the owners of the hot dog stand would not give him one. But then he did something extraordinary and he was given what he asked for.

Thomas Rowley (9)

Shamblehurst Primary School, Southampton

Mermaids

Fabulous mermaids were known for years to
have beautiful hair and tails all different sizes.
Apparently some of them swim around all day in
the deep blue sea, flicking their gleaming tails and
gracefully gliding through the water, while others
comb their silky hair with lovely combs.

Emma Curzon-Tompson (8)
Shamblehurst Primary School, Southampton

The Hiding Friend

Mike hurried upstairs, but when he got there
everything was silent. *Ding-dong!* the doorbell
rang. Mike opened the door. No one was there.
He looked around for five seconds.
'Boo!' His friend Alex came.
'Wow!' Mike said excitedly looking at a parcel.
'Thanks Alex!'

Lucille Nichols (9)
Shamblehurst Primary School, Southampton

186

Empty Space, Or Is It?

'Something's bugging me,' said the astronaut.
'What?'
'Why, there's nothing but holes and space!'
They walked on. Suddenly they saw a UFO. They
floated back to the spaceship as fast as they could.
They heard a voice, 'Capitulate Earthlings!'

Billy Williams (9)
Shamblehurst Primary School, Southampton

Hon The Hot Dog

'Where is this place?' exclaimed Hon the hot dog.
There was a weird noise. 'Chillies!' screamed
Hon. He hated the chillies. The chase was on.
Hon started to squiggle away.
'Hot, hot, hot!' the chillies chanted.
Hon hit something, it picked him up and ate him!

Clayton Parker (9)
Shamblehurst Primary School, Southampton

The Twix And The Mars
Who Both Got Eaten

There was once a Mars walking down the street.
A boy walked along and was about to eat the
Mars but his mum said, 'No, don't eat that.'
Then the Mars ran to the Twix and said worriedly,
'Someone's going to eat me!'
Then someone ate him!

Brandon Spalding (8)
Shamblehurst Primary School, Southampton

Who's There?

Bang! Lily sat up in bed as a shiver went down her spine. The cold unwelcoming room seemed to fill her with dread. She wanted desperately to go home. 'Who's there?' she called, her voice shaking. Something moved, Lily jumped. A scruffy ginger cat came prowling from behind the wardrobe.

Tessa Broadbent (11)

Sherborne Primary School, Sherborne

The Ghost

Tim walked into the garden, he peered through the slimy green window. Suddenly he saw a shiny white ghost. Tim had to keep calm. He ran back into his house screaming! He was terrified. He told his parents but they did not believe him. He was sad.

Cameron Lambert (11)

Sherborne Primary School, Sherborne

It

I got home quite late, went straight to bed. Then I heard my shower dripping. I got up and went to turn it off. I turned the shower off then went back to bed. I heard the phone ring. The wardrobe creaked open. Something bit me. Vampires! Were they real?

Georgia Smith (11)

Sherborne Primary School, Sherborne

A Midnight Smash

The house was silent. It was the middle of the
night. Dollie jumped out of bed, just as she heard
a smash. She ran downstairs to find a vase on the
floor. She was horrified. She turned the light on,
to find her dog, Tess had done it. 'Tess!'

Poppy Harris (11)
Sherborne Primary School, Sherborne

Rumble Rabbit

Alex, the rabbit, was choking on a carrot. Mary was getting worried. Suddenly the rabbit went red as blood. Mary picked Alex up and patted his back and every tap was making Alex calm down and easing the cough. Then Alex stopped coughing and out popped the carrot. A relief!

Lucy Gear (11)

Sherborne Primary School, Sherborne

The Haunter

That night, when my grama went to bed, she heard a noise. It was mysterious. She grabbed her baseball bat and ran to the door. She knocked it down like a bulldozer. It hit the ground with a thump! She found out it was her cat!

Lewis Channing (11)
Sherborne Primary School, Sherborne

A Scary Ride

I was on a roller coaster going at lightning speed.
Twisting and turning, going over and up. A pump
of nausea went round my stomach. As the
roller coaster picked up speed, a hand suddenly
appeared from nowhere - I woke to see the
whole thing was just a dream.

Jamie Hewitt (11)
Sherborne Primary School, Sherborne

Bish, Bash, Bosh

Bish, bash, bosh - 'What was that?' my mum said.
'It could be the builder with me, but he went ages
ago.' *Bish, bash, bosh* - 'That's it, I'm going up.'
Bish, bash, bosh - 'Oh my God!' The head of the
builder was getting smashed on the window by an
escaped prisoner.

Jake Terry (10)
Sherborne Primary School, Sherborne

The Magic Book

I open the book and start reading. Suddenly I'm inside the story! A goblin gives me soup, witches stoop over a seething cauldron. One of them comes to me holding a knife. 'You're next,' she cackles.

Suddenly I'm back in bed. Phew, it was just a dream …

Or was it?

Natasha Jones (10)
Sherborne Primary School, Sherborne

Is It True?

The cake smelt weird. Rhani's parents looked
different. The floor was littered with cigarettes.
I lit my cake. The candle sparked sending smoke
flying everywhere. The candle was soon down to
the bottom. The cake blew up.
'Happy birthday!' they shouted. 'That will take
some money off our food bill!'

William Triffitt (11)
Sherborne Primary School, Sherborne

The Killer Vampire

The boy came to the gate of the haunted house.
The gate creaked open. The creepy-crawlies
ran up his leg. The graveyard guarding the house
really spooked George. He walked down the path
past the tombs. Then the vampire saw George
and ate him. Then he was dead.

Grace Lang (11)
Sherborne Primary School, Sherborne

The Death Cake

I woke up, I saw a cake on my chair. I glared at it for a moment till I went downstairs. Mum and Dad were not there. I went into the living room. The cake was there. It was glaring at me. Suddenly it lunged at me. I was finished.

Rahanur Alom (11)
Sherborne Primary School, Sherborne

In The Room

A boy was living on his own in a house. He opened the door to his room. There was a person playing the piano. 'It's a ghost.' He ran and hid in the corner and stayed there until he died in the corner. He was frozen with fear. Sad …

Brittany Whatley (11)
Sherborne Primary School, Sherborne

Hide-And-Seek

I jumped behind the couch, the creaking of the
stairs, the shadows creeping closer! Every move
made my heart beat faster, every breath was one
closer to death!
'Where are you?'
Oh that voice! It entered the room!
'Found you,' my brother cried.
The game of hide-and-seek was over!

Eleanor Fisher (11)
Sherborne Primary School, Sherborne

203

Untitled

It was a dark gloomy night, a boy called Tom went in the house. It was quiet. As he walked in, he fell into a pit of a million spiders. They were massive. He tried to kill them but he died. It was the end of his life.

Ryan Thayre (11)
Sherborne Primary School, Sherborne

What Was That?

Sarah walked into her bright front door with a cold shiver. Sarah looked at the clock, it was silent. All of a sudden she heard something - *crash!* Sarah ran upstairs like a cheetah. Her heart was pounding, she opened the door. There, in front of her, was her cat, Miny.

Leah West (11)

Sherborne Primary School, Sherborne

205

On The Edge

'Thanks Mum!' I replied. 'Alex. We're going to Alton Towers!'

'What?' cried Alex.

As we passed the gates, Alex and me charged to the Peak. As we clambered onto the Peak we buckled in and braced ourselves. We were thrown into the air. Up and down then *bang!* It stopped.

Lewis Day (11)

Sherborne Primary School, Sherborne

Shadowed Pets

I was outside playing dares when a friend dared
me to go in next-door's house (the resident
had died ten years before). I crept in through
a broken window. There were shadows
everywhere. I heard hissing, then two rough, cold
hands clasped my throat, strangling me. My heart
froze. I died.

Lucy Coleman (11)
Sherborne Primary School, Sherborne

Stranger In The Dark

The streets were dark, there was no light. It was cold. Poppy could not see who the dark figure was staring at her. Then he walked towards her. He grabbed her. It was her dad.

Bree Davey (11)
Sherborne Primary School, Sherborne

Sam Arrived Home

Sam arrived home. *This is unusual,* she thought. There were no lights on. She didn't know what to do. She went to check if the doors were unlocked. She walked in and turned the lights on and then heard a crash upstairs. It was just something that fell.

Jessica Healey (11)
Sherborne Primary School, Sherborne

The Surprise

I opened the door of my house. It seemed quiet,
too quiet. Suddenly I heard, 'Shhh, she'll hear
you.'
I tiptoed to the door. I heard movement. I turned
on the light. I slowly moved my hand to the
handle and opened the door.
'Happy Halloween.'
'Wow, a Halloween party!'

Amber Knight (11)
Sherborne Primary School, Sherborne

In The Dark

My bedroom is scary. *Creak* go the floorboards.
I pull the duvet over me. Suddenly something
comes up the stairs. My heart's beating - *boom,
boom*. The door opens. I scream. It pulls the
duvet off. It's Mum.

Ben Norman (11)
Sherborne Primary School, Sherborne

211

A Frightening Night

A party went on to midnight, until the girl screamed. A hand came up from the floorboards and dragged her under. It took a bite and gobbled her up, then spat her out. She jumped for her friend's hand to pull her out to safety.

Charlie Coombes (11)

Sherborne Primary School, Sherborne

The Dark Mystery

Jack was home alone. He was freaked out and petrified. It was pitch-black. He forgot his mum wasn't coming out of hospital until tomorrow. Suddenly he felt a freeze-like stare. He didn't blink. It was no one. It was painful.
'Ouch for heaven's sake, you idiot.'

Jake Lloyd (11)
Sherborne Primary School, Sherborne

It's Halloween

I was walking at midnight. Monsters everywhere, on my left and right. Ghosts, vampires, zombies and much more. I was without anyone, not anyone; just me and the monsters! Darkness everywhere. No light at all. Just fire glaring out of pumpkin heads, people screaming everywhere. It was most definitely Halloween!

Victoria Hole (10)

Sherborne Primary School, Sherborne

My Babysitter

Suddenly my babysitter sat on me. It wasn't a pretty sight. She played with me like a rag doll. She put me in a baby chair, stuffed a dummy in my mouth. She made me eat this yucky food that babies eat. It was gross. What planet is she from?

Rosie Stephenson (10)
Streatham & Clapham High School, London

Who Is It?

It was the evening. The phone rang but it wasn't
its usual self. I picked it up, 'Hello,' I said. 'Hello,'
I yelled.
Finally I heard something. 'Hhelloo,' coughed a
voice.
I slammed the phone down but suddenly I
realised it was my old uncle, Bean.

Aysha Orchard (9)
Streatham & Clapham High School, London

216

Can Ice Cream Talk?

I heard a voice, squeaky. I thought it was a burglar so I tiptoed downstairs. It was coming from the kitchen. I opened the freezer. I heard a squeaky voice saying, 'Could you take me out?' So I took out the ice cream. It melted slowly in my boiling hot hands.

Lucy Moore (9)
Streatham & Clapham High School, London

Foolish Worm

One gloomy day, a worm was looking down a cliff. Then his glasses fell off and he did not realise, so he went home. On his way home, a dark monster like a shadow appeared from a tree. 'Dinosaur!' the worm shrieked. His friend told him it was a bulldog puppy.

April Adeyinka (9)
Streatham & Clapham High School, London

218

The Pirates

One gloomy day I was strolling along the beach.
A boat popped onto the shimmering waters. As
it rose, massive bubbles appeared on the surface
where I was standing. Suddenly, a pirate came out
of the water and I heard noises. I looked back.
Then a ferocious monster emerged.

Maia Knight-Palmer (10)
Streatham & Clapham High School, London

The Train Driver

The train driver was extremely drunk. He started dancing to 'Poker Face'. Something had gone wrong. We called the police. They started dancing to 'Paparazzi' by Lady Gaga. Suddenly the train crashed. Everyone called the ambulance. They did not care and started dancing. Suddenly the whole train danced to 'Bad Romance'.

Lucy Anthony (9)
Streatham & Clapham High School, London

My Pet Dragon

My mother got me a pet dragon with fangs the
size of my finger and blood-red eyes that glowed
in the dark. He never eats or drinks but he is
cuddly and soft. The one problem is … He's a
toy! But I love my dragon anyway.

Sophie Berman (10)
Streatham & Clapham High School, London

What Pet To Get?

George Griffins awoke with a start. He speculated
which pet to get. 'I know, I'll get a crocodile.'
Sadly the crocodile ate George's mum. George's
dad wasn't happy. The crocodile had to go.
George's second try was to acquire a monkey. He
was just right. George called him Mango Griffins.

Hannah Lea-Gerrard (9)
Streatham & Clapham High School, London

The Rumble

I crept out of my hole, squeezed under the fridge, leapt over a Haribo packet, and I got closer and closer to that horrid rumble noise. I looked to the right and saw the biggest square ever! And it was the washing machine! Inside were my tiny … earmuffs.

Anaïs Watson (10)
Streatham & Clapham High School, London

The Shadow And Sound

I tossed and turned at night. I suddenly woke up, there was a creepy noise. I got out of bed. There was a huge shadow, like a dinosaur, a monster. What should I do? I screamed and heard another noise, it was the same noise. It was my ... cricket.

Macy Guimaraes (10)
Streatham & Clapham High School, London

The Surprise

Suddenly it turned pitch-black. I wandered home.
When I got there, no one was to be seen. It was
my 10th birthday. 'Hello!' I shouted. I crept over
to the living room. My hand slithered up the wall.
I turned on the light.
'Surprise!' voices shouted.
I screamed, then fainted!

Kezia Hayes (9)
Streatham & Clapham High School, London

What Was That Noise?

The clock struck 12. I crept out of the house.
What was that noise? Was it a car zooming past
or a monster coming to eat me? What was that
noise? Was it the rustling of trees or a witch flying
on her broomstick? The noise was a mouse,
scuttling.

Gemma Gurney-Champion (9)
Streatham & Clapham High School, London

Chinese New Year

Bright fiery colours fill the town with joy and friendship. Chinese dragons swooping all around. Beautiful outfits on fair bodies. A dark night with red lanterns in the soft, smooth air. Salty smoke through the town from delicious food. On the rainbow tables families gather together for Chinese New Year.

Madeleine Hayes (10)
Streatham & Clapham High School, London

Ready, Set, Go!

Everything depended on this. I was biting my
nails, even though I wasn't allowed, and shaking
like a rumbling earthquake. Young children were
lined up on the white line. Suddenly a terrible
sound was heard and everyone ran wildly to the
faint finish line. The egg and spoon race began.

Imogen Larkin (10)
Streatham & Clapham High School, London

Will I Ever Get To Sleep?

Will I ever get to sleep? My ears felt like they
had crumbled away. What was that racket, that
horrible noise? My body was aching, my mind was
burning. Suddenly, I felt a longing to know what
it was. I crept downstairs. Finally, I remembered,
we had big, brown mice.

Rebecca Whant (10)
Streatham & Clapham High School, London

The Tramp

Yesterday, I saw a tramp. He caught my eye. His droopy tent and patched up eye. He lives upon trees as night. He sits with his dog on a mouldy piece of log. In a funny sort of way I like him. He seems nice. He's coming to stay.

Jessie-Rose Brown (10)
Streatham & Clapham High School, London

The Soggy Biscuit

Mouse was looking for food. He could see the biscuit tin. He climbed over the obstacles to get there, finally. He pushed open the lid so the gap was big enough for him. He reached in and fell. A hungry person came to get a biscuit. *Crunch* - Mouse was dead.

Millie Minshall (10)
Streatham & Clapham High School, London

Where's My Cookie Gone?

I got a cookie and put it on the table. I went to
get a drink. I came back. My cookie … gone!
It wasn't on the floor. I looked everywhere. It
had been stolen. I walked past the mirror. I had
suspicious crumbs on my face. I'd eaten it already.

Havana Robertson (10)
Streatham & Clapham High School, London

A Very Bad Day

It was a sunny day, I wanted an ice cream. I was boiling. The queue was long. Eventually I got there, the ice cream had gone so I got a lolly. I ran over to my friends, tripped, the lolly flew out of my hand into a huge water fountain.

Constance Griffiths-Clarke (10)
Streatham & Clapham High School, London

The Lost Bunny

There was a young girl crying on her sofa. Her bunny was lost. He was the bunny who always gave her Easter eggs each Easter. She wriggled on the sofa. Then she heard a squeaking noise. She stood up. She had been sitting on her bunny the whole time.

Natasha Watson (10)
Streatham & Clapham High School, London

234

The Four Golden Horses

The horses thundered swiftly across the field into
the dark dangerous night. One wandered too far
until he came to a gloomy cave.
Red eyes stared at him. The monster lashed out. I
woke up. Four golden model horses beside me -
one with a jagged scar across his eye.

Emily Williams (9)
Truro High School, Truro

Royal Nightmares

'Again and again I have the same nightmare,' said
Phoebe. The night her dad went missing. The
king had been dragged right away from Phoebe.
I have to find him, she thought. 'Dad, is that you?'
Phoebe screamed, looking in the shark infested
waters - *Dun, dun dun!*

Tara-Nell Nolan (8)
Truro High School, Truro

The Captain's Boy

There was once a captain who dreamed of sailing on a voyage. He had a crew, but they were always on holiday! One day, a child asked him if he could be in his crew and he became the captain's boy! They travelled the seven seas. It was a great adventure.

Niamh Begley (9)
Truro High School, Truro

In The Life Of A Star

'Yes!' cried Holly as she ran downstairs. 'I'm going to see my favourite band, 'Burn'. I might get backstage tickets!'
'We're here and look, it's starting.' The lights faded but they didn't just play, they chose me to sing with them. It was superb! A night I will never forget.

Keya Patwardhan (8)
Truro High School, Truro

238

The Enchanted Pearl

One day an elegant mermaid was exploring the ocean when she saw a glint in the shadows. A head, a killer whale! She had swam fast, but the killer whale was catching up. One the ground there was a pearl. She touched it and the whale vanished. What a relief!

Chloe Woodrow (9)
Truro High School, Truro

Savannah And Simba The Lions

One day Savannah went out to play in the forest.
She looked up and saw a very fierce dragon. She
shouted! The dragon purred. 'Hang on,' she cried.
She went behind and found it was Simba playing a
trick. 'Simba!' she shouted.
'Sorry,' said Simba. 'Let's go home now
Savannah.'

Amelia Heather (9)
Truro High School, Truro

240

The Powder

When Molly got home she smelled something
coming from the kitchen. She went in and saw
a tall white figure. 'Argh!' She ran and tripped.
The figure bent down with a flannel. 'Stop!' cried
Molly.
'Yes,' said the figure and she put the flannel on
her face. It was Mum!

Hanna Osborne (9)
Truro High School, Truro

The Compound

One day there was an animal in the compound called Berty. He was so jealous because he wanted to go and play with the animals. There was the water hole. He sneaked downstairs and he escaped and had a wonderful time swimming with all the others. What a treat!

Sophie Powell (10)
Truro High School, Truro

Scaly Sea

For the fiftieth time, the powerful tentacle grabbed the mermaid, took her to the seaweed and strangled her. But for a change, it wasn't her father who saved her, it was the prince. They swam back to the castle and she became his princess and lived happily ever after.

Ruth Smith (8)
Truro High School, Truro

Pixie Hollow

At one time in Toadstool Temple lived a stunning pixie princess. She loved adventures. She decided to look for the magical Pixie Hollow. She packed her bag and set off. After so many adventures, she saw the glittering hall. She'd found it! Hidden Pixie Hollow was now hers!

Thea Watkins (8)
Truro High School, Truro

244

Stormy Night

Once upon a time a boat went out to sea. A tremendous storm began. The waves crashed against the rocks. People screamed, people grabbed the sides. The wind howled as the boat bounced up and down. A massive wave carried them to Ireland where they were washed up.

Amy Shaw (9)
Truro High School, Truro

The Halloween Surprise

Sally slowly turned the doorknob and was shocked to find a vampire with shining fangs and blood dripping down his chin. 'Welcome to the Halloween rave!' he snarled.
Sally shivered. The room was full of bloodthirsty creatures. 'Surprise!' all the monsters shouted, pulling off their masks. 'Happy Halloween!'

Issy Geary (9)
Truro High School, Truro

A Day In The Life
Of Someone Different

I woke up screaming and shouting, then sprinted
to my mum and dad's room. It was my birthday!
'Hey, when did you have a makeover?' Mum said.
'You look really different!'
I looked in the mirror and saw I'd turned into Tyra
Banks, my favourite singer and model.

Eleanor Owen (9)
Truro High School, Truro

247

Birthday Dreams

It was coming close to Cindy's birthday. There was one thing she hoped for, a loving velvet pony. She tumbled out of bed. Her parents made her close her diamond eyes and took her outside. She put her hand out and felt something soft. All her dreams had come true.

Ellie Geary (9)
Truro High Shool, Truro

Information

We hope you have enjoyed reading this book - and that you will continue to enjoy it in the coming years.

If you like reading and writing, drop us a line or give us a call and we'll send you a free information pack. Alternatively visit our website at www.youngwriters.co.uk

Write to:
Young Writers Information,
Remus House,
Coltsfoot Drive,
Peterborough,
PE2 9JX

Tel: (01733) 890066
Email: youngwriters@forwardpress.co.uk